I dedicate this book to my children, Bill, John, and Kelly. Nothing gave me greater pleasure than reading to you when you were young, and nothing gives me greater pride than seeing what remarkable adults you have become. Your mother and I feel blessed every day of our lives.

—WHM

With love for the rest of my pack—Rebecca, Rufus, Miles, and Seth.

—HM

About This Book

The illustrations for this book were created with digital paints on an iPad Pro. This book was edited by Deirdre Jones and designed by Saho Fujii and Lynn El-Roeiy. The production was supervised by Patricia Alvarado, and the production editor was Jen Graham. The text was set in Trocchi, and the display type is Bach.

• Library of Congress Cataloging-in-Publication Data • Names: McRaven, William H. (William Harry), 1955– author. | McWilliam, Howard, 1977– illustrator. • Title: Make your bed with Skipper the seal / Admiral William H. McRaven. ; illustrated by Howard McWilliam. • Description: First edition. | New York : Little, Brown and Company, 2021. | Audience: Ages 4–8. | Summary: "Skipper the seal heads to Navy SEAL training and learns ten life lessons (based on the precepts of Make Your Bed: Little Things That Can Change Your Life...And Maybe the World) from his instructors and with friends."—Provided by publisher. • Identifiers: LCCN 2020031719 | ISBN 9780316592352 (hardcover) • Subjects: CYAC: Stories in rhyme. | Conduct of life—Fiction. | United States. Navy. SEALs—Fiction. | Seals (Animals)—Fiction. • Classification: LCC PZ8.3.M42 Mak 2021 | DDC [E]—dc23 • LC record available at https://lccn.loc.gov/2020031719 • ISBNs: 978-0-316-59235-2 (hardcover), 978-0-316-31008-6 (ebook), 978-0-316-30998-1 (ebook), 978-0-316-31019-2 (ebook) • APS • PRINTED IN CHINA • 10 9 8 7 6 5 4 3 2 1

Make Your Bed with Skipper the Seal

Admiral William H. McRaven (Ret.)

Illustrated by Howard McWilliam

Little, Brown and Company

New York   Boston

Skipper the seal lived in the sea.

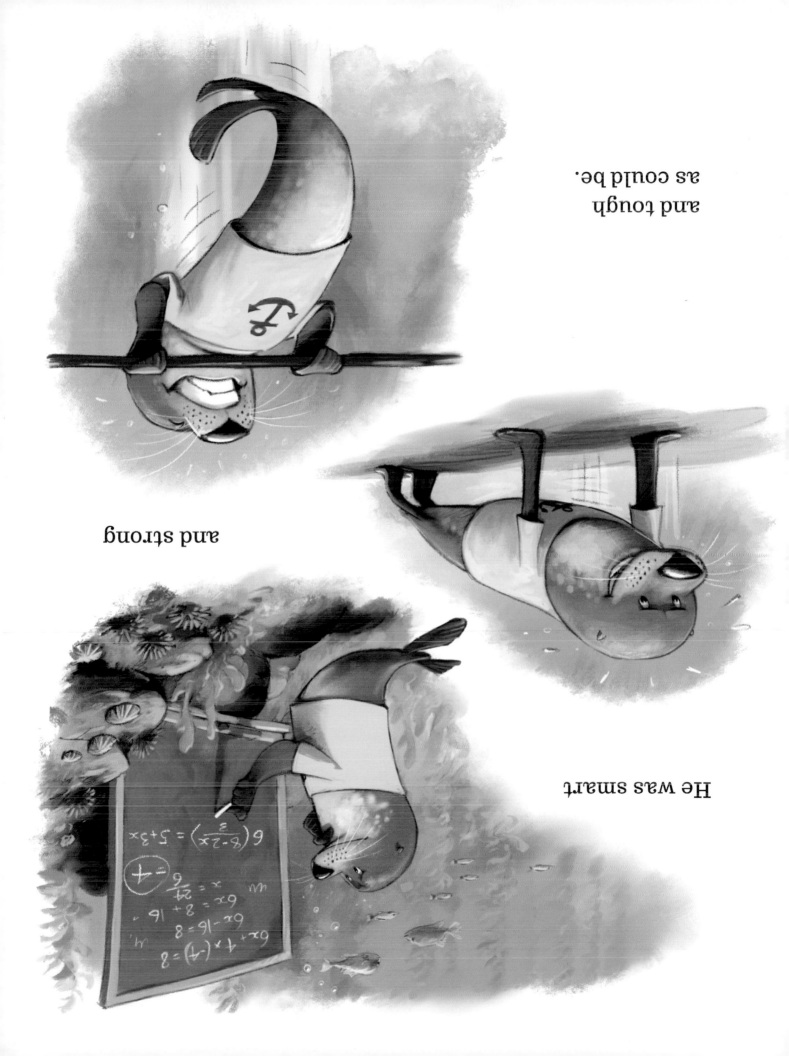

He was smart

and strong

and tough
as could be.

His mom and dad were quite impressed.
Skipper joined the Navy to be the best!

But as he got older, he wanted to leave,
to help his country in times of need.

to be a Navy SEAL!

To go through training, hard and rough,
to find out if he was good enough...

Skipper started each day by making his bed.
"Take a little pride," his instructor said.

"It takes a team,"
the instructor said,
"to conquer the challenges
that lie ahead.

Not one of the seals could paddle alone
and get through the surf to make it back home.

The training was tough, as tough as could be.
Every day Skipper's crew paddled out to sea.

Their size didn't matter, nor did their speed.
All that mattered was their will to succeed.

There were other seals in Skipper's class:
big ones, little ones, slow and fast.

"This teaches the value of doing things right.
It will help you later as you go through life."

"No matter how smart and strong you may be, you will always need friends and family."

Each day the seals had a swimming test
to see which one was the very best.

Skipper reached land before the rest of his pack
and expected a trophy—or a pat on the back.

But the instructor made him roll in the sand
till he looked like a sugar cookie on a baking pan.

"Hard work is important," the instructor said.

"And most days your hard work will get you ahead.

"But sometimes in life, things just aren't fair.
Smile! Don't complain—it won't lead anywhere."

There were times when Skipper was tired and beat

by the training standards he'd failed to meet.

"We all have failures," the instructor said.

"Learn from your mistakes and move ahead."

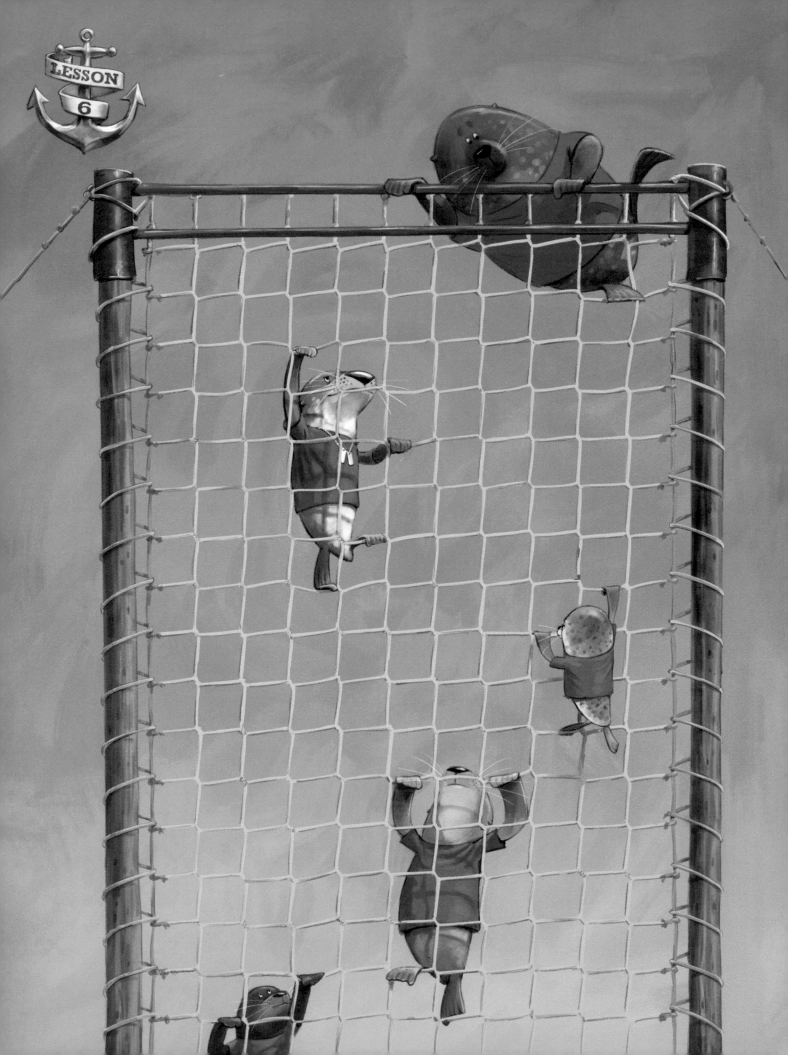

"Now, to be a great SEAL, you must be bold
in your words and actions," Skipper was told.

"Nothing good in life comes without risk.
Don't be afraid, or you might miss…

"...the chance to be great! To make your mark!
To change the world and set yourself apart."

A hard part of training, Skipper soon found,
was when sharks decided to come around.

He asked for advice on what to do,
and his instructor said, "It's all up to you!

"Make sure you remember to *stand your ground*.
That shark is a bully—don't back down!"

Skipper glared at the shark
and stayed proudly in place.

And the shark slunk away
in fear and disgrace.

Next up in training, the pack had to learn
how to dive off a ship from the stem to the stern.

It was dark and scary in the middle of the night,
but like any good SEAL, Skipper shook off his fright.

"You must be your best," the instructor said,
"when things are bleak and there's no light ahead.

"Real heroes are made when life is scary.
Face your fears head-on, and never be wary."

LESSON

9

The toughest week in Navy SEAL training
was down at the mudflats while it was raining.

Skipper and his team had a miserable night.
Their spirits were fading. There was no end in sight.

Then one young seal decided to sing.

For the greatest gift the world has found

Maybe for the others some help it would bring.

is that when things are darkest, hope still abounds.

Navy SEAL training was tough as could be.
But Skipper and his friends were tougher, you see.

They never once thought to ring the bell,
to quit on their team when things didn't go well.

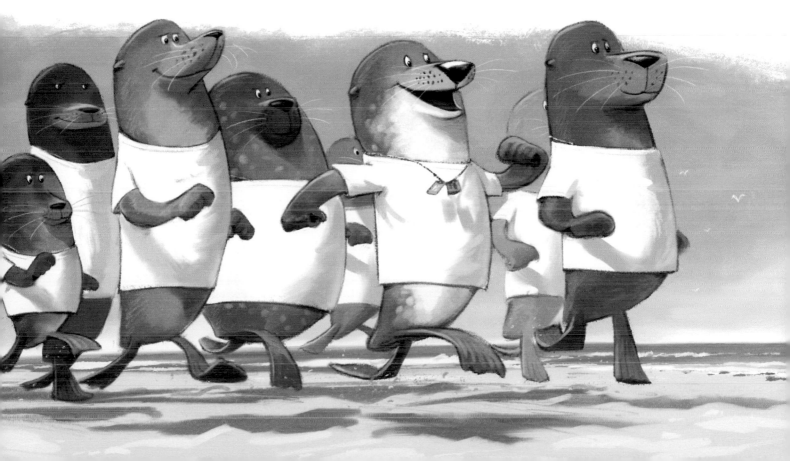

They'd taken SEAL lessons straight to the heart:
Be proud, be brave, be hopeful, be smart!

And Skipper? He'd proven he had the right stuff.
Finally, he *knew* he was good enough...

to be a Navy SEAL!

AUTHOR'S NOTE

After giving a commencement speech at the University of Texas in 2014, I received several requests to write a book outlining the lessons I'd learned in Navy SEAL training, many of which I'd highlighted in my speech. Several years later, I wrote *Make Your Bed: Little Things That Can Change Your Life...And Maybe the World*. In that book, I described how becoming a Navy SEAL taught me to overcome obstacles, to deal with failure, to take risks,* to persevere in tough times; and to become a better person. We all know that life can be very challenging, and whether you're an adult or a young person, the obstacles are often the same. With this new book, *Make Your Bed with Skipper the Seal*, I hope to pass on those same lessons to a younger generation in a way that is both entertaining and uplifting.

* Please always ensure that children have appropriate adult supervision if conducting risky physical activities such as swimming, climbing, or diving.

SKIPPER'S LESSONS

1. START EACH DAY BY MAKING YOUR BED.

2. BE KIND TO EVERYONE.

3. BE A GOOD TEAMMATE.

4. SMILE EVEN IF THINGS DON'T GO YOUR WAY.

5. DON'T BE AFRAID TO MAKE MISTAKES.

6. HAVE FUN AND TRY NEW ADVENTURES.

7. STAND UP TO BULLIES.

8. ALWAYS DO YOUR BEST.

9. BE POSITIVE AND ENCOURAGE YOUR FRIENDS.

10. NEVER GIVE UP. (NEVER RING THE BELL!)